D0968470

CLASH OF THE GLADIATORS

By Catherine Chambers

LONDON, NEW YORK, MUNICH,
MELBOURNE, AND DELHI

DK LONDON

Series Editor Deborah Lock
Project Editor Camilla Gersh
Project Art Editor Hoa Luc
Illustrator Vladimir Aleksic
Producers, Pre-production
Francesca Wardell, Vikki Nousiainen

Reading Consultant
Shirley Bickler

DK DELHI

Editor Nandini Gupta
Art Editor Shruti Soharia Singh
Assistant Art Editor Yamini Panwar
DTP Designers Anita Yadav, Jagtar Singh
Picture Researcher Surya Sarangi
Deputy Managing Editor Soma B. Chowdhury

First published in Great Britain by
Dorling Kindersley Limited
80 Strand, London, WC2R 0RL

Copyright © 2014 Dorling Kindersley Limited
A Penguin Random House Company
10 9 8 7 6 5 4 3 2 1
001—254162—June/2014

A CIP catalogue record for this book is available
from the British Library.

ISBN: 978-1-40934-821-4

Printed and bound in China by South China Printing Co., Ltd.

The publisher would like to thank the following for their kind permission to reproduce their
photographs:
(Key: a-above; b-below/bottom; c-centre; f-far; l-left; r-right; t-top)
4-5 Fotolia: Scanrail (Globes). **4 Dreamstime.com:** Vladyslav Starozhylov (r). **8 Dreamstime.com:** Maksym
Yemelyanov. **11 Dreamstime.com:** Troyka (b). **12 Dreamstime.com:** Rudall30 (tl, tr). **19 Corbis:** Guenter
Rossenbach (br). **20 Getty Images:** Alinari Archives. **21 Getty Images:** Alinari Archives. **24 Corbis:**
Bettmann (b). **25 Corbis:** (t). **26 Corbis:** Pascal Parrot / Sygma (br). **Dorling Kindersley:** Rough Guides (cl).
27 Corbis: Robert Harding Productions / Robert Harding World Imagery (bl); Vanni Archive (cr). **Dorling
Kindersley:** Rough Guides (tl). **28 Dreamstime.com:** Rudall30 (tl, tr). **31 Dreamstime.com:** Maksym
Yemelyanov (bl). **32-33 Dreamstime.com:** Brian Walters. **37 Corbis:** Guenter Rossenbach (br). **40 Corbis:**
Guenter Rossenbach (bl). **44 Dreamstime.com:** Rudall30 (tl, tr). **45 Dreamstime.com:** Vyacheslav Biryukov
(bl). **50 Dreamstime.com:** Maor Glam (t). **50-51 Getty Images:** Richard Bonson. **52 Dorling Kindersley:**
Ermine Street Guard (l). **53 Dorling Kindersley:** The Trustees of the British Museum (cr, bc); Ermine Street
Guard (r). **54-55 Dreamstime.com:** Sgame (Helmet illustrations). **57 Corbis:** Guenter Rossenbach (bc). **60
Dreamstime.com:** Rudall30 (tr, tl). **62-63 Dreamstime.com:** Mexrix. **72 Dreamstime.com:** Krzysztof
Slusarczyk (br). **74 Corbis:** Tarker (c). **74-75 Dreamstime.com:** Maor Glam (Green laurels). **76 Dreamstime.
com:** Rudall30 (tl, tr). **77 Dreamstime.com:** Unlim3d (br). **89 Corbis:** Guenter Rossenbach (bc). **93 Dorling
Kindersley:** The Trustees of the British Museum (cra). **94 Dreamstime.com:** Rudall30 (tl, tr). **99 Alamy
Images:** Jose Ramon Polo Lopez (br). **102 Dorling Kindersley:** Cheuk-king Lo (c/Eggs). **104-105 Dreamstime.
com:** Martina Meyer. **106 Dreamstime.com:** Rudall30 (tl, tr). **108-109 Fotolia:** Derya Celik. **117 Dreamstime.com:** Troyka. **118-119
Fotolia:** Jakub Krechowicz. **119 Dreamstime.com:** Kvasay (br). **120 Dreamstime.com:** Rudall30 (tl, tr).
122-123 Dreamstime.com: Brian Walters

All other images © Dorling Kindersley

For further information see: www.dkimages.com

Discover more at
www.dk.com

CONTENTS

4	Meet the Time Travellers
6	The Location
8	Prologue
12	**Chapter 1** In the Shadow of the Colosseum
28	**Chapter 2** Training for the Ring
44	**Chapter 3** Working for the Gladiators
60	**Chapter 4** Food Fit for Heroes
76	**Chapter 5** Luxury and Treachery
94	**Chapter 6** To Help or to Go Home?
106	**Chapter 7** Escaping the Empire
120	Epilogue
122	Gladiatorial Games Quiz
124	Glossary
125	Index
126	Guide for Parents

MEET THE TIME TRAVELLERS

Imagine that, in a split second, you could be transported to a museum or historical site anywhere in the world. Well, a group of young history enthusiasts turned the dream into reality, creating a unique club called Secretly Living in the Past (SLIP). Together they developed a mobile app that transports them to museums and historical sites anywhere on the planet. That is anywhere and whenever they wish...

SETH: in Cornwall, England
He is interested in the Roman period, especially the Romans' curious lack of interest in colonising Cornwall.

HIROTO: in Kyoto, Japan
Hiroto is passionate about ancient languages. He is trying to develop a translator app.

ABRINET: in Axum, Ethiopia
She is also interested in the Romans, especially their impact on Africa.

5

MAP KEY

Roman Empire

Roman Arenas

Britannia
(England)

Durnovaria
Dorchester, England

Noviomagus
Chichester, England

Oceanus Atlanticus
(Atlantic Ocean)

Gaul (France)

Burdigala
Bordeaux, France

Verona Augusta
Verona, Italy

Nemausus
Nîmes, France

Hispania (Spain)

Carthago Nova
Cartagena, Spain

Thysdrus
El Jem, Tunisia

THE LOCATION

Across the vast Roman Empire,
awesome amphitheatres fill with crowds.
People gather to listen to poets reading
odes and to watch actors performing
plays. The thunder of chariot races and
sparring beasts thrill them, but they
wait restlessly for the main event: the
gladiators! This is the era in which our
time-travelling team find themselves...

Pietas Iulia
Pula, Croatia

Roma Colosseum

Pontus (Black Sea)

Italia
(Italy)

Ulpia Serdica
Sofia, Bulgaria

Asia (Turkey)

Macedonia
(Greece)

**Roma
Colosseum**

Rome, Italy

Aezani
Çavdarhisar, Turkey

Antiphellos
Kaş, Turkey

Mare Internum (Mediterranean Sea)

Leptis Magna
Khoms, Libya

Aegyptus (Egypt)

PROLOGUE

"Want 2 SLIP?" Seth texted Abrinet.

"Where 2?" Abrinet texted back.

"Colosseum – Rome. Great guided tours of the gladiator school ruins!"

"OK!"

Seth thought a bit before he texted her again. Should he tell her, or shouldn't he? Seth just couldn't hold back.

"Got a surprise Abri."

"What?"

"I adapted the app – speeded it up."

"Yeah, whatever."

"No, really – race you 2 Rome!"

"I'm eating. Ethiopia 2 hrs ahead – OK? C u in half hr."

Seth leaned back on the swivel chair in front of his computer screen. He stretched and yawned. Plenty of time.

Seth stared at the new app on his mobile's screen. He was desperate to try it out but hesitated, turned on his computer and clicked on the SLIP app creator icon. Scrolling through the dense lines of script, he entered the destination software. Then he opened up the file holding some programming ideas. Seth hovered over one that was particularly tempting. Well... why not? His fingers copied lines of script onto his new app programme. The fresh instructions went straight to the mobile app through the computer link.

"Okay, I'll see if that changes the destination coordinates." Seth smiled slightly wickedly to himself.

"Yep. If I press the star key once and the hash twice, I should now land just to the side of the Colosseum. Ha! Ha! I'll be in exactly the right place to surprise Abrinet!"

Seth checked the time on his mobile and texted Abrinet.

"SLIP in 30 secs."

"OK."

Seth searched his pocket and took out his lucky Roman coin. He flipped it with excitement. Looking at it, Seth remembered how he had found it beneath a tall, tapered stone on the family farm. The coin was a bit battered and had a small nick on one edge. No one knew how it got there, and no amount of digging had found any other evidence of Roman occupation. Seth shrugged.

Never mind. Soon he would immerse himself in the Colosseum of ancient Rome – well, the ruins of it.

5-4-3-2-1. Star-hash-hash. Seth's fingers fumbled. Hash. NO! An extra hash! In that split second, Seth's whole body weakened. He knew he might have made a shocking mistake...

CHAPTER 1
IN THE SHADOW OF THE COLOSSEUM

"WAAAGH!" Seth gasped. His body lay slumped across a deep, circular brick washtub. Seth looked down into the grey water. It absolutely stank of urine. He pulled his head away in disgust and jerked his body upright. The scene around him was strangely familiar, but only from Internet pictures of ruins – and these were no ruins.

A row of the washtubs divided by low partitions covered in limestone slabs was set against a wall and shaded by a neatly tiled roof. The space was open on one side, and along it, shallow, rectangular troughs were set into the ground.

Strong men stood in them, stamping the clothes so hard that the rinsing-water gushed through ceramic pipes and down the narrow city street. Boys pummelled clothes clean in the tubs of urine.
The thump of their feet, the sound of sloshing water and the piercing shouts and laughter made Seth feel dizzy.
He crouched down behind a stout brick pillar and listened hard. He could hear names – shouted loudly.

"Heus! Petrus!... Hanno!... Aurelio!" There was also a lot of, "Puer! Heus!"

"Puer. Puer?" Seth remembered. It was Latin for 'boy' – usually yelled at slaves. Phew! That was one thing he recognised.

Seth's heart was racing – so was his brain. Well, he seemed to be in Rome, so the new coordinates he had computed had worked. Yay! What was going on, though? Seth suddenly smiled to himself. His body relaxed and he curled up laughing.

"A film set! Yes, that's it. I'm on a film set! If I stay back and keep quiet, I'll have a great view of the whole thing!"

Seth's mobile rumbled. Oh no, Abrinet. He had totally forgotten about her.

"WHERE R U?"

"Outside Coloss. Join me. Star and two – no, three – hash keys."

"3? OK."

Seth gazed upwards, a bit anxious about Abrinet's landing. He was right to worry as he watched her horrifying crash to earth – straight into a man carrying a huge, circular wicker basket frame perched upside down over his head.

Clothes were laid over it, sparkling white and dry. All of them fell to the ground, and the man screamed with rage, not knowing what had hit him. Seth grabbed Abrinet, hauling her into the washhouse.

"OOOPH!" she gasped. "What kind of landing did you programme, Seth?" Somehow, Seth could tell she wasn't pleased.

"You're okay, aren't you? Keep your voice down or we'll get thrown off the set."

"The set? What set?"

"A film. We're in a film. By the Colosseum. Just look around you. Look at the detail."

Abrinet drank it all in. In the street outside the open-sided washhouse, a boy of their age was sweeping away heaps of donkey droppings. Men weaved around him carrying baskets on their

16

heads piled high with fruit, vegetables and herbs. The man she had bumped into was returning with another wicker frame – a bit like a cage. He set it down over a clay pot. Then he took a pile of damp, white clothes and strung them around the frame.

"It's a clothes whitener!" Abrinet explained to Seth. "The pot's got sulphur in it. It's heated up, and the sulphur steam helps to bleach the clothes. Wow! The researchers have really done their homework!"

Seth noticed a small boy struggling to hang some gigantic tunics on a line.

"I bet those enormous white woollen tunics belong to gladiators."

"Hmm. Maybe," replied Abrinet, studying a boy smoothing out the woollen fibres with a stiff wire brush.

"D'you think they'll be filming gladiators in the Colosseum?"

"I reckon," said Seth. "We could go and watch. Actually, we don't need to watch. We can join the extras in the crowd. We stand out with these clothes on, though. Look! There are some small tunics in a pile behind that pillar."

"And loincloths hanging not far on that clothesline, too," pointed Abrinet.

They both giggled at the thought of wearing long loincloths wound under their tunics – just like the Romans.

"Great for hiding our mobiles," pointed out Seth. "I expect they're banned on set."

Abrinet and Seth pulled on their Roman clothes and stuffed their 21st-century gear under a massive pile of togas waiting to be washed. Then they strolled out slowly from behind the pillar, staring at the scene all around them. Abrinet looked puzzled.

"Okay, Seth. So where are the cameras?"

Seth shrugged. "They must be on a crane somewhere, or attached to those arched windows high up on the Colosseum."

Seth and Abrinet looked up and gazed long and hard. Their mouths hung open, vulnerable to the frenzy of flies that swarmed around the urine pots set at street corners, waiting to be taken to the washhouse.

?
What clues would you expect to see if Abrinet and Seth were on a film set?

ALL DRESSED UP

Men

The basic dress for men in Rome was a tunic. The type of tunic worn showed others what social class they belonged to. Citizens also wore togas over their tunics.

Hair
Roman men traditionally cut their hair short and were clean-shaven.

Tunic
This was a simple white garment worn with a belt.

Toga
This was draped carefully over the shoulder and tucked in at the waist. Only the emperor could wear a purple toga.

Sandals
Most people wore sandals, although some people wore closed leather shoes.

S. P. Q. R
RINVENUTA· NEL· VIALE· PRINCIPESSA· MARGHERITA
IL· XVI· AGOSTO· MDCCCLXXIX

Women

Unlike men, women had no way of indicating their social status through their dress, though they wore a variety of colours. A married woman wore a stola, while an unmarried woman wore only a chiton.

Hairstyle
Women's hairstyles in Rome were very elaborate.

Belt
Women sometimes wore a belt over the chiton.

Chiton
This was a garment made up of two large pieces of fabric tied together at the shoulders.

Palla
When women went outside, they wore this cloak.

"The Colosseum," whispered Abrinet. "It's... it's intact. No ruins. And... and the stone and concrete are for real – really... truly... real. No hardboard. All completely genuine."

A muscle-bound fullo, a washerman, carrying a tall, heavy pile of enormous creamy-white woollen tunics strode towards them.

"Ite ad Ludum Magnum!" he boomed, dumping the tunics in front of them. "NUNC!"

Seth and Abrinet did not need to speak Latin to understand that he wanted them to take the clothes. They hurriedly divided the pile between them, struggling under the weight.

"Ludus Magnus – I understood that bit. The Gladiator School. Told you these were gladiators' clothes! I think he wants us to take the clothes," Seth muttered.

"You're scoring points on whose clothes they are?" stormed Abrinet. "What planet are you on? We're stuck in ancient Rome – for real – and as much as I love it, I'd like to go home some day and see Mum and Dad and my little brother. Now follow me, because I bet you didn't study the tourist map or the Colosseum diagram before you left. We need to access the Ludus Magnus through a passageway from the Colosseum, or we'll get stopped by the guards at the school's entrances. Here we go!"

Colosseum Opens with Great Fanfare

The highly anticipated Flavian Amphitheatre has finally opened with a magnificent ceremony in Rome.

Emperor Titus inaugurated 100 days of games, which he dedicated to the people of Rome. The games will include gladiatorial contests, battle reenactments, animal hunts, executions and drama productions.

"We must thank the gods for our mighty empire, but without the hard-working and brilliant people of Rome, none of this would be possible," the Emperor said. "And so it is not the gladiators, the senators, nor even me, your emperor, whom we honour today. Instead, we celebrate the gods, and of course, you, the Roman people."

Many of the Emperor's critics have argued that the games serve merely as a distraction for the recent Vesuvius disaster and the terrible outbreak of plague in the city.

The construction of the amphitheatre began ten years ago, under the Emperor's father, Vespasian. Built of concrete and stone, it is capable of holding up to 80,000 spectators, making it the largest amphitheatre in the Empire.

Gaius Sempronius Sciavola, the chief builder on the project, said, "It has been a long and arduous process, but I think everyone will agree that it was worth the wait and the effort. It really is a building all of Rome can be proud of."

The first day of the games was well attended, with every seat in the amphitheatre filled and even more hopeful spectators queuing up outside to get in. One visitor, Marcus Antonius Creticus, said, "I've never experienced anything like it. The atmosphere is amazing here. I've never been more proud to be a Roman."

The games in the coming days are sure to present some magnificent spectacles, with a reenactment of the naval Battle at Zama planned and appearances from some of the Empire's greatest gladiators, including Priscus and Verus.

LET'S GO!

CULTURAL TOURS OF THE ROMAN EMPIRE

Visit some of the Empire's most impressive arenas!

PIETAS IULIA

More than 26,000 spectators can enjoy the events at Pietas Iulia. The amphitheatre's four side towers make this a magnificent example of Roman architecture.

NEMAUSUS

The Nemausus amphitheatre is one of the largest in Gaul, capable of holding 24,000 spectators. Here you can watch some of the finest gladiators in all the provinces.

VERONA AUGUSTA

Visitors come from all over the world to see the world-famous gladiators at this spectacular arena. Its white and pink limestone make this a beautiful sight.

THYSDRUS

The Roman Empire's third-largest amphitheatre can hold up to 35,000 spectators. It is located in one of Africa's wealthiest and most important cities.

ANTIPHELLOS

Enjoy the rustic charm of this old Greek amphitheatre. A trip to the eastern provinces would not be complete without enjoying the sea views from its steps.

CHAPTER 2
TRAINING FOR THE RING

Abrinet marched off in front, her knees buckling under the mound of tunics and elbows knocking into the street-food sellers as she went. Behind her, Seth stared longingly at the platters of bread – hot and yeasty and topped with poppy seeds. Some were square, others round. Red earthenware pots held steaming soup with floating aromas of chickpeas, garlic and herbs: rosemary, mint and thyme.

Seth thought wistfully of Cornwall's grassy cliff tops with their carpets of wild, aromatic plants.

Abrinet swerved suddenly and dived through a small open entrance at the side of the Colosseum. She descended carefully down a dark stairwell, then stopped.

"Seth," she panted. "Let's figure out how to get out while we're in a quiet spot. How about reversing your app – you know, the star and hash thing?"

"I've thought about it," whispered Seth, bundling the clothes on top of him. "I don't think that'll work. I just don't know where we'd end up – probably in the same place, but even deeper in time, I suspect. I need to think..."

"Okay. Then we must find a way of knowing what's going on here and now. And we need to be able to talk our way out of any trouble. Latin. We need more Latin." Seth and Abrinet looked at each other and smiled.

"Hiroto!" they declared together, high-fiving at the same time.

"I'll text him," said Seth. "What time do you think it is in Japan?"

"He won't care. He'll be up all night programming, anyway."

Seth took his mobile from a fold in his loincloth and began texting.

"Hi Hiroto! Abri 'n' I need help! How's ur language app doing?"

"Hi u 2! Y? Bet u in trouble, huh?"

"Just a bit."

"App nearly there. Want 2 test it."

"Test it on us! We need Latin."

"R u joking? OK then. But don't blame me... Get ready 2 receive app, both of u."

"Then what?"

"Follow instructions. I need 2 know if they work OK. Gd luck!"

Abrinet and Seth looked at the app.

"Test it on me!" Abrinet insisted. "Set it to my local language, Tigrinya. Open the mike, then the translator, and I'll speak. Let's see if we get it in English."

"K'mal ka?" she asked Seth.

"How are you?" A bland, robotic voice translated it instantly into English. Abrinet nodded and smiled.

"That'll be fine," Seth said with confidence. "Let's set it to Latin and turn the sound down." Seth and Abrinet then tucked their mobiles under folds of cloth on their shoulders, close to their ears.

Seth and Abrinet stepped from the alcove into the stone-floored passageway and strode towards a long shaft of light ahead.

It drew them into a vast, noisy, oval arena. Marble pillars supported an open, arched cloister all around, with rooms and corridors running off it.

Muscled gladiators sat around the cloister, talking. Some peered through entrances into the arena, studying others practising their skills or shouting out advice – or warnings. A gladiator broke from his training and drank thirstily from a stout, triangular stone water fountain set at one end of the arena. A trainer's assistant emerged from a large room hung all around with weapons and armour. He strolled over to a gladiator and fitted him with shiny arm- and shoulder-pieces.

A citizen dressed in a fine toga over a blue tunic called out from the elite north-facing section of the stepped cavea – the seating area around the arena. He was a lanista, a gladiator-trainer or manager. From his dress, Abrinet and Seth could tell that he was a very successful one.

"Why that arm-piece?" called out the lanista.

"His opponent's left-handed and wields a double-sided axe," replied the assistant.

The man sat down again and muttered to his friends, throwing his arms in the air, a large gold ring glistening on a finger.

Seth and Abrinet stood mesmerised.

"Hey!" shouted a man from a room set back from the arena. "You two! Get over here with those tunics! I've been waiting since noon for them! Where've you been? Watching those illegal dice-throwers, I'll bet! They'll be gambling with their lives if they're caught. Everyone knows you don't gamble until the feast day, and that's not 'til tomorrow."

Seth and Abrinet put the clothes down in the dark room piled high with laundry.

"I'll get you to take some dirty laundry back to the fullones later," the man barked. "They've got all the rich praetors' clothes to wash for tomorrow's great spectacle, so we've got to wait in the queue. Now would you believe that, eh?"

He laughed sarcastically, then pointed admiringly at two gladiators resting at the side of the arena.

"See those two gladiators over there? Off to the restaurant with you and fetch their lunch – lanista Titus Fabius has ordered it specially. Those gladiators are stars. Real stars. They won't put up with the food from the kitchens in here, I can tell you! Just make sure you say it's for Titus Fabius – and it's the special diet."

"Special diet," whispered Abrinet as they hurried over to the two gladiators.

"Mmm," agreed Seth. "Like Olympic athletes back home. This is all so interesting."

"I'm glad," Abrinet replied. "Stops me from thinking about..."

"Back home," Seth finished the sentence for her.

?
Use the Internet to research the diet of Olympic athletes.

THE GLADIATOR TRAINING SCHOOL

The Ludus Magnus, the Great Gladiatorial Training School in Rome, was the world's largest and best school for gladiators. Here the most famous gladiators lived and trained.

A

Gladiators' living quarters

Most gladiators were slaves. Some were even criminals, so they lived in small quarters like those in a prison.

C

Cavea (seating)

Many people enjoyed watching the gladiators practise. They sat in seats surrounding the practice area, which were reserved for specific social classes.

B

North entrance

This was reserved for important spectators and visitors.

D

Hypogeum

To make it easy for gladiators to enter the arena, this tunnel connected the school to the Colosseum.

Fountain
The gladiators relied on this fountain to get all the water they needed.

Colosseum (Flavian Amphitheatre)
The gladiatorial school had the best possible location, right next to the Colosseum.

SPEAKING THE LANGUAGE

The language the Romans spoke is called Latin. Join in the conversation between these two Roman citizens.

Soldier
Salve O Caesar!
Hail Caesar!

Caesar
Confecistine opus tuum?
Have you finished your work?

Soldier
Minime, Domine.
No, sir.

Caesar
Qua ratione?
Why not?

Soldier
Canis opus meum consumpsit.
My dog ate my work.

Caesar
Tace! Mendax et ignavus es!
Be quiet! You are a liar! You are lazy!

Soldier
Me paenitet, Caesar!
I am sorry, Caesar!

ROMAN TIMES

CLASSIFIED ADVERTISEMENTS

42

WANTED

Young slave girl needed to serve meals and help the lady of the house with other tasks

MINE WORKERS

Hard-working, strong slaves required for gold mine in the north of Italy
All inquiries welcome

DANCING GIRLS WANTED

Must be graceful

Excellent prices offered

Immediate start

SECRETARY

Greek- and Latin-speaking secretary needed to assist prominent merchant

Offer price on application

EXPERIENCE THE GLORY OF BEING A GLADIATOR!

Fighters of all experience levels needed

Fantastic benefits

HELP REQUIRED

Nanny needed to look after three children, ages 5, 7 and 10

SERVICES

GREAT DEALS ON SLAVES!

Thoranius can cater to all your slave needs
Children of slaves, prisoners-of-war and criminals available

Best slaves in town!

Gargilianus's slave dealership offers only slaves of the highest quality
All slaves are thoroughly checked for diseases, injuries and lice
Visit us at the Forum Magnum

CHAPTER 3
WORKING FOR
THE GLADIATORS

Seth and Abrinet did not get very far.

"Hey!" yelled another man carrying armour and weapons. "Go over there and get this armour cleaned!" He pointed to a tiled area in front of the armoury and close to the two chatting gladiators. "Gleaming. That's what this armour has to be. Gleaming. It's ceremonial – not your everyday wear. Just remember!"

Seth and Abrinet wanted to say they had already been asked to fetch the gladiators' lunch but decided against it. They stared at the armour. There was a lot of it.

"Chain mail," said Seth, spreading out two huge coats of upper-body armour. "It's the scales type – bronze, too, not iron. Those gladiators must be stars! I suppose I shine it up with this mixture." He sniffed at a pot of liquid and then handed it to Abrinet.

"At least it's not urine! Mmmm. Vinegar probably. Dare you to taste it, Seth!"

"UUURGH! That's disgusting! Vinegar, with a heap of salt in it," said Seth, spitting it out. Abrinet laughed.

"I should use it on these helmets, too," she said. She polished the Gallic helmets until they gleamed, taking special care over the embossed patterned ridges at the base of the helmet and the beautifully decorated cheek guards.

The work was hard on their arms and the cleaning mixture stung their fingers after a while. Seth was careful not to wet the cloth onto which the small bronze scales were sewn. He was amazed to find gold thread worked between some of the lines of scales.

Abrinet discovered that the embossed decoration on the cheek guards was silver and that the broad neck guard was the dirtiest and took a lot of her energy. For a while, though, both she and Seth were able to forget their situation. In sight of the arena, they were awed at the skills of the gladiators practising for their big day.

"They're more like actors rehearsing for a play," decided Abrinet, "just practising sequences rather than belting each other or that pole in the middle."

"They need to make sure they can move in their gear okay, I suppose," pondered Seth. "I mean, look at that guy over there, covered in armour."

Seth pointed to a secutor, whose heavy, scaled, fish-like armour slowed his movement so that his strides were

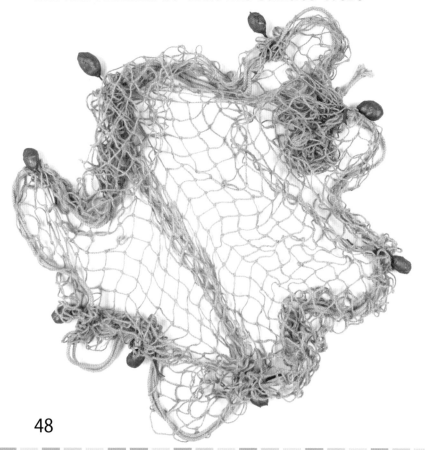

laboured as he lunged with his left shoulder, his right hand wielding a gladius – a short sword. Long cloth padding strapped on with leather ties protected his arms. An assistant entered. He carried a huge hemp-rope net, made heavy with lead weights sewn around the edge. It was an iaculum, which the assistant practised throwing over the secutor with one hand, the other holding a long, rectangular shield, curled inwards, to fend him off.

"It's like playing out a scene at sea, with the fisherman trying to catch the guy in the armour – as if he's a mighty shark or something," said Seth.

Tomorrow the real fisherman gladiator, the retiarius, would be wielding a dangerous trident. The secutor would try to attack him before he could be netted, wounded by the trident and finished off with the retiarius's dagger.

GLADIATOR HIGH SCHOOL

Welcome to the Ludus Magnus, the Great Gladiatorial School in Rome! Here you will receive the best-possible training to become a gladiator. We'll teach you how to fight, how to entertain and how to die.

NAME: **SPICULUS**

GRADE: **NOVICE**

LANISTA: **TITUS FABIUS**

TIMETABLE

6:30–7:30   Fitness training

7:30–9:30   Introduction to sword-fighting

9:30–11:00   Defence for beginners

11:00–13:00   Introduction to spear-fighting

13:00–13:30   Lunch

13:30–15:30   Fancy footwork

15:30–17:30   Performance: entertaining
              the audience

17:30–19:00   Preparing to die with honour

19:00–20:30   Dinner

20:30–22:00   Bathing and massage

LETHAL WEAPONS

Gladiators had special weapons and wore specific armour. Though their armour was different from soldiers' armour, it was just as important.

GALERUS
Shoulder-piece

BALTEUS
Belt

GLADIUS
Sword

OCREAE
Shin guards

GLADIUS
Sword

GALEA
Helmet

SCUTUM
Shield

JAVELIN

53

KNOW YOUR GLADIATORS!

Get to know each type of gladiator and other important participants in the games.

Venator

SPECIAL ABILITY
Animal-hunting

WEAPONS
Spear, darts, javelin

OPPONENTS
Wild beasts

ARMOUR
Usually none, wearing only a loincloth

Paegniarius

SPECIAL ABILITY
Making the crowds laugh

WEAPONS
Wooden sword, whips, nets

OPPONENTS
Other paegniarii

ARMOUR
No helmet, shield or other armour; only protective wrapping on legs and head

Murmillo

SPECIAL ABILITY
Sword-fighting

WEAPONS
Rectangular shield; sword

OPPONENTS
Thraex, hoplomachus, retiarius

ARMOUR
Heavy linen wrapping on right arm; shin guard on leg; helmet with a fish-like crest

Hoplomachus

SPECIAL ABILITY
Fighting with a lance

WEAPONS
Small, round shield; lance; short, straight sword

OPPONENTS
Murmillo

ARMOUR
Long shin guards; heavy linen wrapping on the right arm; helmet with a tall crest

54

Thraex

SPECIAL ABILITY
Close-contact fighting

WEAPONS
Short sword with an angled blade; small, square shield

OPPONENTS
Murmillo

ARMOUR
Long shin guards; helmet decorated with feathers, with a tall crest in the shape of a griffin

Provocator

SPECIAL ABILITY
Close-contact fighting

WEAPONS
Curved, rectangular shield; short sword

OPPONENTS
Other provocatores

ARMOUR
Helmet with no crest; breastplate; heavy linen wrapping on right arm; shin guard on left leg

Retiarius

SPECIAL ABILITY
Fighting with a net and trident

WEAPONS
Trident, net, short sword

OPPONENTS
Secutor, murmillo

ARMOUR
Heavy linen wrapping on left arm; shoulder-piece on the left side

Secutor

SPECIAL ABILITY
Defence against a trident

WEAPONS
Curved, rectangular shield; sword

OPPONENTS
Retiarius

ARMOUR
Heavy linen wrapping on right arm; shin guard on left leg; smooth helmet with a small crest and tiny eyeholes

Seth and Abrinet jumped, as ghastly cries echoed from the centre of the arena. They peered through the entrance and reeled back in horror and disgust.

A gladiator attacking the central pole with a small round shield had fallen and speared himself with a slender, leaf-shaped dagger. Deep-red blood gushed from his upper arm. Two other sparring gladiators ran towards him. Titus Fabius, the man with the glistening ring, hurtled down the steps yelling, "Take him to his cell! I'll fetch my own surgeon! How can this have happened? I bet he slipped. I blame that sandal-maker using thin leather for the soles. That's my feast day ruined!"

"He should have paid to have them studded with hobnails, then. What d'you think, Bryon?"

They turned from the sickening blood-soaked scene and listened hard.

Over the piercing shrieks in the arena, Abrinet and Seth heard the mighty gladiators speak for the first time.

"You're right there, Negash. Our lanista's got a mean streak sometimes – always expecting his gladiators to work miracles in the arena. Typical!"

?
How would you describe the scene and action around the injured gladiator?

"Bryon! That's English!" whispered Seth excitedly.

"And Negash is... I'll tell you later." Abrinet stopped as she saw the man who gave them their cleaning job striding towards them. In his arms lay a large bundle of arrows and elegant but lethal bows made of bone and wood.

"Should we clean their weapons?" asked Abrinet.

"Clean their WEAPONS?" yelled the man. "No one, but NO ONE touches those weapons but ME! D'you get it? How do I know you're not going to tamper with them, eh? What are you — slaving for some spy or something?" He threw some stones at them.

"Get out of here!"

Seth and Abrinet ducked and turned towards the southern exit but were stopped in their tracks by the man who asked them to fetch the gladiators' lunch.

"Hey! You two! I thought I told you to get them their lunch from the taberna! Go on, get lost!"

"Yes, get lost, and get yourselves some snacks, too!" said the gladiator called Bryon, tossing some coins down at their feet. The two gladiators roared with laughter at Seth and Abrinet's bewildered faces.

CHAPTER 4
FOOD FIT FOR HEROES

Seth and Abrinet wandered up and down the street, not knowing how to find the taberna. What was it like? A street stall? A barbecue? They were so hungry they couldn't think straight, so they stopped to buy food from a snack vendor.

"Two chickpea soups and some square bread – the ones with poppy seeds on them, please," said Seth.

"You're lucky," the vendor remarked.

"That's the last serving. And you wouldn't want to buy your lunch at the lanistae's taberna over there. Prices are as inflated as a consul's ego – and his bloated stomach!"

The trainers' taberna! They were right on track. Seth and Abrinet stood in front of the large, open-sided restaurant crammed with customers eating at tables or sitting on stools. On the right, a huge L-shaped stone stove puffed plumes of steam from enormous, heated pots sunk into one side. On the floor of the taberna stood a bronze oven, with boiling water steaming and frothing from pots inside. A chef shovelled bread and pizzas into another oven set into the wall behind the stove.

"Yes?" asked the chef.

"Please, we've come to collect an order for Titus Fabius," said Abrinet. "Special diet." She had only just remembered!

FOOD FIT FOR FIGHTERS

Today's menu offers our chef's seasonal selection, made from only the freshest ingredients sourced from Rome's best markets. Our menu is specially planned to provide our gladiators with all the nutrients they need.

Today's Menu

BREAKFAST

Oatmeal porridge

•

Barley porridge with dried figs and dates

LUNCH/DINNER

All served with barley bread

•

Polenta with chickpeas and vegetables

•

Chickpea stew with cabbage and leeks

•

Lentil stew with barley and onions

SIDES

Assorted olives

•

Roasted vegetable medley:

cabbage, cauliflower
and broccoli

•

Char-grilled asparagus

•

Summer salad:

lettuce, onions, artichokes and
cucumbers drizzled with vinaigrette

DESSERT

Dried fig and date assortment

DRINKS

Ash milkshake:

made with your choice of plant ash,
bone ash or a combination

The chef nodded and dished up two huge platters of polenta with a heap of vegetables and chickpeas surrounded by a salad of green leaves and olives.

"There. No meat. Tell Titus Fabius we're sorry we served up meat the other day. I thought a good chunk of chicken would put some muscle on them, but apparently it burns them out. All those diet experts. Pah!"

Seth and Abrinet thanked the chef and began walking carefully back to the Ludus Magnus. Seth stopped at a wall above a bookshop full of papyrus scrolls. Painters were just finishing a fresco on it: an advertisement for the following day's spectacle at the Colosseum.

"Abrinet – what did you want to say earlier about that gladiator's name – uh – what was it?" Seth asked.

"Negash. If I'm not mistaken, it's from my part of the world. It means 'born to be king'."

Seth read out the Latin words painted on the advertisement.

"Look! It's talking about two gladiators, and it says, 'Marcus, from Axum. Captured while on a trade mission to the city of Rome. Thought to be a spy for his father, the king'."

Abrinet continued, "And then it says, 'Quintus, captured in Britannia while fighting against Imperial Rome. His grandfather fought with the notorious Boudicca. Two daring foreigners. Now mighty gladiators'. They must be our gladiators for sure, just with the Roman names given to them by their captors."

"And there's the date, so now we know what time we're in!" added Seth.

"Tomorrow is 15th March 125CE. We're in 125CE! That's Hadrian's reign. If only we weren't trapped here, this would be awesome."

Seth and Abrinet returned to the Ludus Magnus determined to find out more about Bryon and Negash, but as soon as they had delivered the food, the trainer's assistant appeared.

"Hey! You two! Get over here! Took your time, didn't you? You're needed in the cell of that wounded gladiator. There's blood all over the floor. Get it cleaned up."

Seth and Abrinet followed the assistant into the kitchen, where a woman handed them buckets, sand, a jug of vinegar and some old woollen cloths. Seth and Abrinet cleaned up the blood and then stood back, watching the surgeon at work.

"He needs to be calmed down. Give him some henbane!" ordered Titus Fabius.

The surgeon stared at him coldly.

"I'll be using a small piece of mandrake. It'll deaden the nerve endings and help with the pain. It will also slow his heart rate and control the bleeding."

The surgeon was soon removing a piece of the dagger, which had broken off and stuck into the gladiator's humerus, or arm bone. Using an ivory-handled scalpel, he opened up the wound a bit more and then popped the piece of dagger out with a bone drill. He teased out small chips of bone with the vulsellum, a pair of forceps. Acetum, a vinegar antiseptic, sterilised the wound. The two sides of jagged skin were lined up neatly together with a hamus actus hook. It was all over.

"There. Keep up the vegetable and herb diet," advised the surgeon. "It'll help the healing process."

"You can go." Titus Fabius motioned Seth and Abrinet away.

Seth shook his head. "It really isn't much of a life being a gladiator."

"I don't know – just look in there!" replied Abrinet, pointing to a gladiator lying down in his cell, his muscles being massaged and oiled. The scent of perfumed oils wafted through the cloisters: marjoram to calm him, lavender for his aching muscles, geranium to balance the mind and body and jasmine to uplift his spirit. Seth and Abrinet started walking yet again towards Bryon and Negash.

"Hey! Not so fast!" It was Titus Fabius. "Follow me to the bathhouse!" he commanded. "I need to wind down and clean off this filthy blood spattered all over my skin."

Abrinet and Seth turned around. As they passed a side entrance to the arena, they glimpsed two gladiators sparring furiously.

"It's the woman in the kitchen who gave us the cleaning stuff!" exclaimed Seth.

"Yes. I saw a gladiator's tattoo on her hand but didn't think it was for real!" replied Abrinet.

The woman was lightly protected with a wide leather band around her waist, a bronze chest plate, ocrea shin guards and padded arm protectors. She was agile and fast, thrusting her shield in defence against the longer sword of her opponent, and then dabbing dangerously at the arteries under the other woman's neck and behind her knee.

"I wish we could stay and watch," grumbled Seth. "I can't think of anything more boring than slaving in a bathhouse for that spoiled diva of a trainer."

"Hmm. I think we should be careful about using the word 'boring'," warned Abrinet.

TOP TREATMENTS

Roman medicine relied on a range of natural products to treat illnesses and heal wounds. Some of their remedies are still in use today.

Fennel was thought to stem the flow of blood from wounds.

Henbane was used as an anaesthetic and painkiller.

Lavender was thought to have soothing properties.

Elecampane could be used to relieve aches.

Garlic was taken to support general health and was also used as a disinfectant.

Sage was a powerful healer, sacred to the Romans, and used especially to treat sore throats.

Rosemary was part of the treatment for coughs, wounds and skin problems.

73

THE FIVE GREATEST GLADIATORS

SPARTACUS

Spartacus had been a soldier, a slave and a gladiator. In 73BCE, he led a slave revolt, beginning in the gladiatorial schools in Capua, Italy. He managed to raise a powerful army of more than 70,000 men and had many victories against the Roman military.

COMMODUS

Commodus was the emperor of Rome from 180 to 192CE. He loved the gladiatorial games and became infamous as the first and only emperor to fight as a gladiator.

FLAMMA

Flamma was such a successful fighter that he was offered the rudius — a wooden sword symbolising freedom — four times. Each time, he rejected it and continued to fight until he died at the age of 30.

CRIXUS

Crixus was Spartacus's second in command during the slave revolt. He and Spartacus had met during a fight, when Spartacus refused to kill him after he had been defeated. They remained friends until Crixus's death in 72BCE.

PRISCUS AND VERUS

Priscus and Verus were great rivals. A fight between them was one of the highlights of the opening games at the Colosseum. They were so popular that the Roman writer Martial wrote a poem about them.

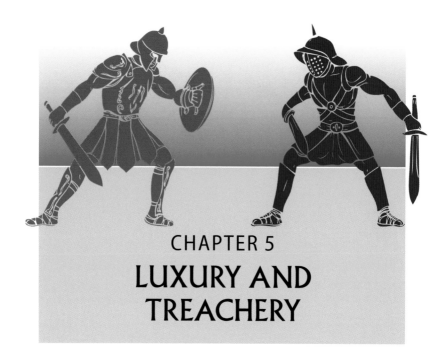

CHAPTER 5
LUXURY AND TREACHERY

Seth and Abrinet trailed through the city carrying piles of woollen towels and fresh clothing for the lanista. The narrow streets finally opened out onto a grassy area that led to an enormous building of marble and concrete. It was positioned to catch the most of the sun.

"It's got to be Trajan's baths," observed Abrinet, "and if I were going to spend hours with wet skin, I'd want as much sun to warm me up as possible."

Inside the impressive building, they passed by a gymnasium, reading room and theatre, and headed straight for the baths. On the way, Seth and Abrinet marvelled at the marble columns of the colonnade at the centre of the building, the tiled floors and mosaics and the tall, leafy plants. Frescoes of gods and goddesses lined the walls.

They reached the shiny tepidarium, with its bronze benches and beautiful blue glass that made the water glisten.

ROMAN BATHS

All Romans visited public baths. People used the baths to get clean, but they were also places to socialise.

Natatio

Palaestra

BATH ACTIVITIES

Natatio

For a little exercise before the bath, people could go for a swim in this outdoor swimming pool.

Palaestra

Other activities, such as running, boxing or handball, were enjoyed in the exercise yard.

Women's tepidarium

Women's caldarium

Men's caldarium

Men's tepidarium

Men's frigidarium

Caldarium
The bathing began with a visit to this hot steam room.

Tepidarium
In this warm room, slaves rubbed oil into the skin.

Frigidarium
The trip finished with a stop in the cold room and a dip in a refreshing bath.

At the baths, Titus Fabius calmed down a bit in the lukewarm water. By the time he reached the caldarium, with its scalding water and steam areas, he was almost happy. Then an attendant arrived with a message.

"Excuse me, sir. Senator Publius Cornelius Crispus wishes to meet you in the scraping room at sundown."

The lanista's face fell. He started muttering to himself.

"Oh, I don't believe it! Senator Publius is the sponsor for tomorrow's contest. He's heard about that idiot gladiator's accident already. It's wrecked his programme, I'll bet."

Titus Fabius growled, demanded several towels and made his way hastily to the scraping room, with Seth and Abrinet following behind.

"Ah, Titus Fabius!" cried the senator warmly. "Wonderful to see you! All set for tomorrow?"

"Well, Senator Publius Cornelius Crispus, I expect you know all about gladiator Lucius's most unfortunate accident. He is such a dedicated fighter..."

"Yes, yes," interrupted the senator.

"No matter. We needed extra time anyway. I have a little plan for the end of the programme – for the Briton and the Ethiopian."

Seth and Abrinet looked up and listened keenly.

"That's Bryon and Negash!"

"Marcus and Quintus? They're in good shape," smiled Titus Fabius. "They trained early this morning, and they've been resting all day. We can look forward to a good demonstration to finish off the evening. The crowd love them."

"Ah yes," replied the senator. "Demonstration. That's what I wanted to discuss. Tomorrow's umpire, here, is going to join in."

The umpire, Felix, greeted the lanista with a curt nod of the head, and the senator continued.

"The thing is this, Titus. Tomorrow, as you know, is the Ides of March — the great festival of Jupiter and of Anna of Perenna. Our beloved Emperor Hadrian will be attending. It is a great day for us all."

The other two men nodded in agreement.

"Moreover, four days after that, the Feast of Minerva will hit the streets of Rome. Our skilled artisans will drop their tools for five days to honour their patron saint. Then, of course, it will become an excuse for militant slaves to rampage, party and complain."

"So what we need, Titus, my friend, is a killing at the Colosseum – a gift to the Emperor, the crowds in the arena and the ungrateful slaves."

Titus Fabius looked at him nervously. "Surely, Senator Publius Cornelius Crispus, you are not suggesting that one of my best gladiators should die? Those two have entertained crowds for years with their amazing demonstrations. Where will I find another such pair? I've got others who I'd happily kill off – well, for a fee of course. We lanistae always need our sponsors to compensate us for a financial loss."

"Oh, I know the game, Titus! I will make it well worth your while. You'll be able to retire on the amount I'll be offering."

The senator whispered a figure behind his hand.

"Mmm," replied the lanista, reflecting on how the senator had fallen badly out of favour with Emperor Hadrian.

"Of course, Senator. I suppose a killing will get you back in our emperor's good graces. He does at least understand how a good killing shows dedication to the people, even if he doesn't like it, so..."

The senator sighed and whispered another figure behind his hand – twice that of the first. Titus Fabius agreed.

"The plan is this: the gladiators will gallop into the arena on horseback as usual and perform their display. Then they will dismount and spar with each other. Bows and arrows will be involved in a true Sagittarian spectacle, and as we know, the crowd usually joins in – there will be arrows flying everywhere. It will be a perfect camouflage for our paid marksman. No one will even notice him.

"You are to ensure, Felix, that the gladiators spar within his line of fire. The marksman will shoot at the same time as one of the gladiators. He will aim for the neck, so no neck guard, Titus."

The conversation soon ended.
The three men lay down on the bronze benches, where attendants scraped off the oils used to wash their bodies with strigils. These carved ivory-handled scrapers looked a bit like paper knives, Seth thought.

"Careful with those strigils!" said the senator. "Remember what they say happened to our great Emperor Augustus's face – covered in revolting sores. Too eager with the strigil!"

They all laughed once more.

Titus Fabius went to the frigidarium, but decided to skip the massage. He felt more cheerful now. Soon he would be a very rich man indeed.

Any anxiety he once felt now fell upon Abrinet and Seth. They could not wait to return to the Ludus Magnus. Bryon and Negash had to be warned, but why would they listen to a pair of slaves?

?

How would you convince Bryon and Negash to listen to your story about the plot to kill them?

PRAISE THE GODS!

Within the Roman Empire, people were devoted to hundreds of gods. However, there were a few very important gods to whom everyone prayed.

Mars

God of war

Jupiter

King of the gods and sky god

Vesta

Goddess of the home

Juno

Goddess of women

Venus

Goddess of love
and beauty

Apollo

God of the sun, healing
and music

Mercury

Messenger of the gods and
god of merchants

Minerva

Goddess of
crafts and war

ROMAN CALENDAR

The calendar we use today is based on the Roman calendar, so there are many similarities. The names of our months come from the names of Roman months, and each had the same number of days as our modern months.

Roman name	Modern name	Days in the month
Ianuarius	January	XXXI
Februarius	February	XXVIII
Martius	March	XXXI
Aprilis	April	XXX
Maius	May	XXXI
Iunius	June	XXX
Iulius	July	XXXI
Augustus	August	XXXI
Septembris	September	XXX
Octobris	October	XXXI
Novembris	November	XXX
Decembris	December	XXXI

FEAST DAYS

The Romans did not have weekends. These were only introduced when the Romans converted to Christianity in the 4th century CE. Until then, their days off work were the feast days, when they could come together to spend time with their friends, family and neighbours.

Equirria
This was a chariot-racing festival in honour of the god Mars. It was held on 17 February and 14 March.

Feast of Anna Perenna
The Feast of Anna Perenna was on the Ides of March (15 March). It celebrated springtime and new beginnings. It also coincided with a festival dedicated to the god Jupiter.

Quinquatrus
Quinquatrus was a festival in honour of the goddess Minerva. It began on 19 March and continued for five days. The first and most important day was the dedication of Minerva's temple. Subsequent days consisted of gladiatorial contests, plays, speeches, poetry and the consultation of fortune tellers.

Kalends, Nones and Ides
Romans divided the months using Kalends, Nones and Ides. The Kalends was the first day of the month; Nones was eight days before the Ides; and the Ides was in the middle of the month.

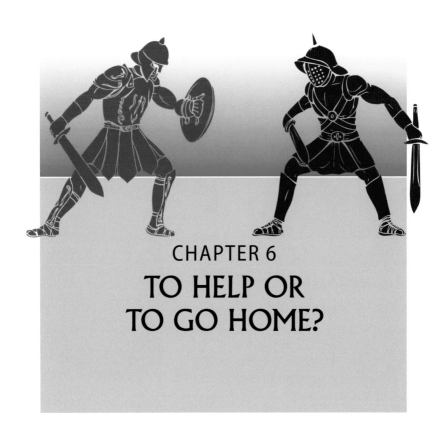

CHAPTER 6
TO HELP OR TO GO HOME?

Abrinet and Seth trailed Titus Fabius back to his house bearing damp towels. They entered the Ludus Magnus just as the light was fading. Lamps shone along the shaded cloisters, but there was still one last eager, or desperate, training assistant barking out orders in the arena.

"Go forwards and attack! Okay. Now, he's attacking back and you need to retreat. No! No! No! Not to the left! That's what he's expecting. You're always coming in from the right and retreating to the left. Next time, try leaping back in exactly the same way as you leapt forwards..."

Seth stopped in his tracks.

"Slow down, Abrinet! Just for a second. I've got the answer – at least, I'm pretty sure I have. We can go home! Abrinet, we can GO... HOME!" His eyes shone with relief.

"How?" whispered Abrinet, hardly able to believe it.

"That trainer just then, he said, 'Try leaping back in exactly the same way as you leapt forward.' Well, that's it! That's what we have to do. Star – hash, hash, hash! Exactly the same code that brought us here. It'll take us back!"

"You're amazing, Seth Trewyn!" smiled Abrinet, reaching for the mobile under her shoulder strap. Then she stopped and shook her head.

"No. You're right. We can't," said Seth. "Not yet."

Abrinet swallowed nervously, knowing that the battery on her mobile was running low. She put her thoughts aside, though, and the two marched off with determined steps towards Bryon and Negash, choosing the dangerous path.

In a quiet corner of the cloisters, Bryon and Negash sat together, eating from a platter of barley, beans and dried fruit.

"What do you two want?" asked Bryon roughly as Seth and Abrinet approached them. Abrinet decided that the direct approach was the best.

"Tomorrow," she said, "one of you will die. The sponsor, the umpire and your lanista, Titus Fabius, have arranged it between them. The one to die will be shot with an arrow by a trained marksman."

The two enormous gladiators fell about laughing.

"Okay," said Negash. "That was great entertainment." He tossed them some coins. "You've earned yourselves another good meal."

Seth and Abrinet's faces remained serious. Seth picked up the coins and put them down by Negash's side.

"We don't want your money. We want to help you escape and maybe even find a way to go home."

The two gladiators stopped eating and started listening to the conspiracy that had played out in the baths of Trajan.

"How do we know we can trust you?" asked Bryon. "Many people before you have offered to help us and turned out to be traitors. We had to have them killed."

"Because we've got nothing to gain," said Seth. "We've just refused your money and you can't free us."

"And we know where you're from, so we know how much you'll want to go home," added Abrinet.

The two gladiators sent Abrinet and Seth away. They needed to talk and plan. It was dark when they called Abrinet and Seth to their sides. They snuffed out the torches to avoid attention and revealed their plan to Seth and Abrinet.

Bryon handed a huge pile of coins, tied up in a blood-stained tunic, to Seth and Abrinet. No one would suspect what was inside. A coin dropped and Seth picked it up.

"Keep it to buy yourselves breakfast," Bryon said.

The two gladiators turned towards the cloisters and their sleeping cells.

"This is a very sad day for us," said Negash, shaking his head. "We are close to retirement and have earned enough money to live in luxury. Grand houses that we ourselves have paid for are just waiting for us."

Seth and Abrinet left them and made their way through the streets of Rome, knocking on doors and whispering instructions. When their mission was complete, Seth and Abrinet returned to the Ludus Magnus. There, they found a warm spot near a charcoal fire by the kitchen. In the light of the embers, Seth pulled the Roman coin that Bryon had given him from his loincloth. He stifled a cry.

"Look, Abrinet! A picture of Hadrian on one side and Britannia on the other. And a nick in the side! It's... it's just like mine!"

"Don't be ridiculous; you've pulled out the wrong one," replied Abrinet grumpily, trying to sleep.

Seth foraged in his pocket and picked out his own coin. It was identical. The two of them stared in disbelief until tiredness took over, and they slept until early morning.

A BAGFUL OF MONEY

The first Roman coin was called the as. It was made of bronze and introduced in about 290BCE. The as would remain the coin with the least value as the sestertius, denarius and aureus were introduced.

Almost everyone in ancient Rome used the denarius for money.

WHAT PEOPLE EARNED

Wall painter	75 denarii per day
Barber	2 denarii per customer
Bath attendant	2 denarii per customer
Carpenter	50 denarii per day
Farm labourer	25 denarii per day
Manual labourer	25 denarii per day
Scribe	20 denarii per 100 lines
Stonemason	50 denarii per day
Teacher	200 denarii per month
Baker	50 denarii per day

WHAT MONEY WOULD BUY

Whole beans 60 denarii per modius

Beef or mutton 8 denarii per libra

Cheese 8 denarii per libra

Chickens 60 denarii for 5

Eggs 1 denarius each

River fish 8–12 denarii per libra

Olive oil 40 denarii per sextarius

Wheat 100 denarii per modius

Approximate equivalents   Modius = 8.5 litres/16 pints
Libra = 330 grams/11.5 ounces
Sextarius = 550 ml/1 pint

Toiling for the Empire

JOB DESCRIPTION

Job title
Lanista

Location
The Great Gladiatorial Training School, Rome

DESCRIPTION

The lanista is in charge of every aspect of a gladiator's life, from the moment he joins the school to his death or retirement. The lanista will look after exercise and training programmes, diet and rest.

Main duties

1. Developing training programmes and routines and supervising gladiators' training

2. Caring for gladiators' injuries, referring serious injuries to the surgeon

3. Managing the training of new lanistae

SKILLS, KNOWLEDGE AND EXPERIENCE

Essential

1. Prior experience of working with gladiators or soldiers

2. Knowledge of weaponry and battle tactics

3. Patience and good communication skills

Desirable

1. Some experience of teaching

2. A basic understanding of medical treatment

3. Knowledge of nutrition

OTHER FACTORS

Hours of work: 6.30 a.m.–10.00 p.m. daily

Salary: 50 denarii per day

Holiday: five feast days per year

Other benefits: accommodation and food provided

CHAPTER 7

ESCAPING THE EMPIRE

Seth and Abrinet awoke to the sound of heralds outside, calling out the glad tidings of the Feast of Jupiter. Fanfares trumpeted to citizens and slaves alike: "Come and enjoy the great spectacle at the Colosseum!" The streets were packed with sellers crying out their wares.

Spectators, around 50,000 of them, poured along the streets leading to the Colosseum. Seth and Abrinet hung back by a slaves' entrance, clutching their tickets and watching. Slaves and women scrambled along the vomitorium – the aisle that led to their places. Beneath them, soldiers and ordinary citizens jostled for seats. Below, with a much better view, were the equestrians – important government officials. Passing through the north gate, magistrates and senators in their fine togas took the best seats of all. Finally, and with great fanfare, Hadrian himself appeared and settled in the emperor's box. The show was about to begin.

Seth and Abrinet climbed near to the top.

A GREAT DAY OUT

Eighty pairs of gladiators provided by Publius Cornelius Crispus, Roman senator, will fight at the amphitheatre in Rome on the Ides of March.

✦ ✦ PROGRAMME ✦ ✦

<u>Morning</u>

Opening Parade

✦ Entry of the Vestal Virgins ✦
These sacred priestesses will be accompanied by priests, senators, soldiers and musicians.

✦ Entry of the Emperor ✦
He will be accompanied by the umpire, arms, armour and horses to be used, as well as by musicians, acrobats and the palm-bearer.

✦ Entry of the gladiators ✦
Enjoy your first look at the day's competitors.

✦ Hunting display ✦
Rome's finest beast-fighters will hunt ostriches, giraffes, wild boar, buffalo, cheetahs, elephants, lions and leopards.

Noon

Midday Games

> ✦ **Executions** ✦
> Deserters, prisoners-of-war and criminals
> will be crucified and thrown to the lions.

✦ **Mock fights** ✦
Clowns will perform mock battles that will
have you rolling in the aisles!

Afternoon

✦ **Weapons** ✦
Inspection of the weapons and armour
will be conducted by the umpire.

✦ **Gladiatorial bouts** ✦
Eighty pairs of gladiators, including
hoplomachi, murmillones, provocatores,
thracians, retiarii, secutores and sagitarii
will go head-to-head. Among the star
fighters, you will see Priscus, Verus,
Flamma, Tetraites, Marcus and Quintus.

✦ **The Battle of Zama** ✦
Witness a spectacular reenactment of
the crushing naval defeat of Carthage.

"Look like you're part of the crowd," Negash had advised, "and when gladiators are at the end of their fight, don't shout, 'Mitte! Let him live!' Shout, 'Lugula! Kill him! Kill him!' Then no one will be suspicious of you."

Seth and Abrinet tried to appear enthusiastic about their day at the Colosseum, and at first they were. Musicians played, and acrobats and wrestlers entertained the crowds, while assistants pulled lavish pieces of scenery into their final places.

"It's like being in a gigantic theatre," Abrinet observed. "Look at the trees, bushes and grassy hills."

"Never mind that. Look at the elephants and giraffes! And the big cats!" Seth cried. "Over there! Leopards – and a lion. And another – and cheetahs!"

"No, DON'T look!" cried Abrinet. "See those hunters hiding behind the scenery

with bows and arrows and spears?
It's going to be revolting!"

Seth and Abrinet closed their eyes.
The cries echoing around the arena
deafened their ears. Then rain came
and the crowd hushed as men yanked at
pulleys. A great awning spread out above
the arena, protecting the spectators from
the rain.

Soon, animals and scenery were
whisked away and on came the
gladiators. There were eighty bouts in
all, with contrasting styles and weapons.
Gladiators wore their best armour,
embossed with silver and gold. Seth and
Abrinet opened their eyes when they
realised that there were certainly some
nasty wounds but no kills.

Seth studied the umpire and his
assistant, as they looked closely at every
move, occasionally halting the fight for
reasons that Seth could not understand.

"I can't follow the rules. They're too complicated," complained Seth.

"The bouts are so short that it's hard to fathom them," agreed Abrinet. "The gladiators' helmets are too heavy and they can't fight for long. Have you noticed? The first thing they do after a contest is take them off and move their necks around."

Abrinet followed the programme closely until the secutor and retiarius appeared in the arena – the fabulous fisherman spectacle that Abrinet and Seth had witnessed in the Ludus Magnus.

"We have to go now," said Abrinet. "It's the last event before Bryon and Negash's finale... and our final act." She shivered a little at the enormity and truth of it all.

Seth and Abrinet slid away and slipped out of a slaves' entrance. They raced to the east gate, mingling with the street sellers. The soldiers guarding the gate kept looking around, talking to each other anxiously and watching a woman and a small boy, who were hovering suspiciously.

Then the Colosseum erupted with roars as Bryon and Negash's horses thundered through the hypogeum – underground passages from the Ludus Magnus.

Galloping up into the centre of the arena, the two gladiators fought in a well-rehearsed mock display. Swords clashed, armour buckled, arrows flew – it looked so real. The umpire waved a discreet signal with his hand. It was time for the two horsemen to dismount and continue their battle on the ground.

Bryon and Negash turned quickly towards the east gate, the Gate of Life, and galloped towards it. Officials and ticket marshalls screamed and fled as the horses threw them aside. At the gate, the guards looked around.

"Where's this money we were promised to open the gate?" shouted the head guard in total panic.

Just as Bryon and Negash galloped into view, Seth and Abrinet dashed forwards and thrust two pouches stuffed with coins into the face of the head guard. He laughed triumphantly, pulled

the gate open, and ran off with
the others – and the money.

The woman and small boy nervously
waiting at the edge of the crowds outside
the Colosseum ran forward, calling out to
the two horsemen. With joy, Bryon
pulled up the woman, his wife, onto the
back of his horse. Negash lifted the small
boy. The boy was Negash's son.

Just as they all prepared to flee, Seth
thrust a coin into Bryon's hand.

"Take it!" he cried. "It's lucky – believe
me! And don't forget, when you reach
Britannia, go west to Cornwall. It's safer
from the Romans there. I have an old
Cornish name for you, too – Govan.
It means 'sparrow'."

The gladiator roared with a long,
deep laugh, and then disappeared.

Seth and Abrinet mingled with the
crowd that stood stunned at the sight
of the two escaping gladiators.

"Time to SLIP," said Abrinet.

Moving into the shadows of a quieter street, they pulled out their mobiles. Their batteries were very low now.

"What if they run out while we're mid-SLIP?"asked Abrinet. "Will we just float around in the middle of nowhere? Will it be like... dying?"

"We can't afford to think about it," said Seth. "Come on. Together now."

"5-4-3-2-1. Star. Hash-hash-hash."

Odes to the Greatest Gladiators

To the Romans, gladiators were great heroes. Some Romans admired them so much, they even wrote poetry about them.

Ode to Marcus of Axum

Hail Marcus of Axum, our winner!

A prisoner praised by Rome

Ever since he was a beginner.

In the arena he roamed,

His only wish to go home.

Ode to Quintus of Britannia

Quintus! The noblest of fighters!

From a mighty barbarian clan,

The favourite of this writer.

Quintus is a fearless man.

True, I am his biggest fan.

EPILOGUE

"R u ok?" Abrinet texted Seth, now safe at home in Axum. Seth texted back.

"OK. Mum wants 2 know where my clothes r!"

"Wonder what Romans thought of your T-shirt with 'I love London' and a red bus on it!" replied Abrinet.

"Ha ha! Seriously – should we do it again?" texted Seth.

"Star. Hash-hash-hash? You bet!"

"Wonder what happened 2 Bryon and Negash."

Seth and Abrinet would never know. After their escape from the Colosseum, however, Negash and his young son took a trading ship to Carthage in North Africa, then on to Alexandria. From there, they sailed down the Nile to Axum, their home.

Bryon and his wife galloped across to France and then on to England. Along the way, Bryon worked as a freelance gladiator in the arenas of Arles, Bordeaux, Chichester and Dorchester. Finally, they stopped on a wild, windswept headland in Cornwall, England, where they settled and became farmers. In a corner by a wall, Bryon dug a deep hole. He dropped in his lucky coin and covered it over with a tall, tapered stone.

Gladiatorial Games Quiz

See if you can remember the answers to these questions about what you have read.

1. What clue let Seth and Ábrinet know that they were not on a film set?

2. In what year was the Colosseum completed?

3. How did Seth and Ábrinet understand the language the Romans were speaking?

4. What language did the Romans speak?

5. What did Seth and Ábrinet use to clean the gladiators' armour?

6. What kind of gladiator uses a net as a weapon?

7. What makes a gladiator's diet so special?

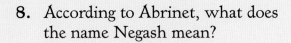

8. According to Ábrinet, what does the name Negash mean?

9. When did Spartacus lead a slave rebellion?

10. What did the Romans use henbane for?

11. Which room in a Roman bath house was steamy?

12. What was the name of the Roman goddess of war?

13. How many months did the Roman calendar have?

14. What was the name of the most common type of coin in Rome?

15. Who was the woman waiting nervously at the edge of the crowds during the gladiatorial games?

Answers on page 125.

GLOSSARY

cloister
A covered walkway that looks onto a courtyard through rows of columns.

colonnade
A long row of columns in a building.

consul
A high-ranking official in the Roman Empire.

fresco
A type of wall painting in which the paint is put on to wet plaster.

marksman
An archer who is very good at shooting.

mosaic
A floor or wall decoration made from small pieces of glass, stone or tile cemented into position to make a picture or pattern.

papyrus
A paper-like sheet made by pressing the stems of reeds together, on which documents were written.

praetor
A high-ranking Roman lawyer.

strigil
A tool used by the Romans to scrape oil and dirt off the skin.

taberna
A Roman shop or restaurant.

Vestal Virgins
Roman priestesses who worshipped the goddess of the home, Vesta.

INDEX

amphitheatres 6–7, 24–27, 39, 108
Colosseum (Flavian Amphitheatre) 7, 8, 10, 11, 16, 17, 19, 22–25, 30, 38, 39, 65, 75, 85, 106, 110, 113, 115, 121, 122
armour 33, 44, 45, 48, 49, 52–53

baths 70, 71, 76–81, 98

calendar 92–93, 123

diet 36, 37, 61–64, 68, 104, 122
dress 20–21, 34, 35, 42, 107

feast days 35, 56, 83, 93, 105, 106

gladiators, famous 74–75
Spartacus 74, 75, 123
gladiators, types of 54–55

gods and goddesses 24, 77, 90–91, 93, 123

lanista/lanistae 35, 36, 50, 57, 61, 76, 80, 83, 85, 86, 97, 104–105
Latin 13, 22, 30–32, 40–42, 66
Ludus Magnus (Great Gladiatorial School) 8, 22, 23, 38–39, 50–51, 65, 67, 89, 94, 100, 104, 113

medicine 72–73
money 98, 99, 102–103, 114, 115

ode 6, 118–119

slaves 13, 38, 42–43, 74, 75, 79, 83, 85, 88, 106, 107, 113, 123

weapons 33, 44, 52–55, 58, 105, 109, 111, 122

Answers to the Gladiatorial Games Quiz:
1. The Colosseum was intact; **2.** 80CE; **3.** They used Hiroto's translator app; **4.** Latin; **5.** Vinegar and salt; **6.** Retiarius; **7.** It has no meat; **8.** Born to be king; **9.** 73BCE; **10.** As an anaesthetic and painkiller; **11.** The caldarium; **12.** Minerva; **13.** 12; **14.** Denarius; **15.** Bryon's wife.

Guide for Parents

DK Reads is a three-level interactive reading adventure series for children, developing the habit of reading widely for both pleasure and information. These chapter books have an exciting main narrative interspersed with a range of reading genres to suit your child's reading ability, as required by the National Curriculum. Each book is designed to develop your child's reading skills, fluency, grammar awareness and comprehension in order to build confidence and engagement when reading.

Ready for a *Reading Alone* book

YOUR CHILD SHOULD

- be able to read independently and silently for extended periods of time.
- read aloud flexibly and fluently, in expressive phrases with the listener in mind.
- respond to what he/she is reading with an enquiring mind.

A VALUABLE AND SHARED READING EXPERIENCE

Supporting children when they are reading proficiently can encourage them to value reading and to view reading as an interesting, purposeful and enjoyable pastime. So here are a few tips on how to use this book with your child.

TIP 1 Reading aloud as a learning opportunity:

- if your child has already read some of the book, ask him/her to explain the earlier part briefly.
- encourage your child to read slightly more slowly than his/her normal silent reading speed so that the words are clear and the listener has time to absorb the information, too.

Reading aloud provides your child with practice in expressive reading and performing to a listener, as well as a chance to share his/her responses to the storyline and the information.

TIP 2 Praise, share and chat:

- encourage your child to recall specific details after each chapter.

- provide opportunities for your child to pick out interesting words and discuss what they mean.

- discuss how the author captures the reader's interest, or how effective the non-fiction layouts are.

- ask the questions provided on some pages and in the quiz. These help to develop comprehension skills and awareness of the language used.

- ask if there's anything that your child would like to discover more about.

Further information can be researched in the index of other non-fiction books or on the Internet.

A FEW ADDITIONAL TIPS

- Continue to read to your child regularly to demonstrate fluency, phrasing and expression; to find out or check information; and for sharing enjoyment.

- Encourage your child to read a range of different genres, such as newspapers, poems, review articles and instructions.

- Provide opportunities for your child to read to a variety of eager listeners, such as a sibling or a grandparent.

Series consultant **Shirley Bickler** is a longtime advocate of carefully crafted, enthralling texts for young readers. Her LIFT initiative for infant teaching was the model for the National Literacy Strategy Literacy Hour, and she is co-author of *Book Bands for Guided Reading* published by Reading Recovery based at the Institute of Education.

Here are some other
DK Reads you might enjoy.

Terrors of the Deep
Marine biologists Dom and Jake take their deep-sea
submersible down into the world's deepest, darkest ocean
trench, the Mariana Trench.

Pony Club
Emma is so excited – she is going to
horseback-riding camp with her older sister!

In the Shadow of the Volcano
Volcanologist Rosa Carelli and her son Carlo are caught up in
the dramatic events unfolding as Mount Vesuvius re-awakens.

The Mummy's Curse
Are our intrepid time travellers cursed? Experience ancient
Egyptian life along the banks of the Nile with them.

Ballet Academy
Lucy follows her dream as she trains to be a professional
dancer at the Academy. Will she make it through?

Galactic Mission
Year 2098: planet Earth is dying. Five school children embark
on a life or death mission to the distant star system of Alpha
Centauri to find a new home.

Twister: A Terrifying Tale of Superstorms
Jeremy joins his cousins in Tornado Alley for the holiday.
To his surprise, he discovers they are storm chasers and has
the ride of his life!